characters created by lauren

Boo! MADE you jump!

PUFFIN

Text based on the script written by Dave Ingham

Illustrations from the TV animation

produced by Tiger Aspect

PUFFIN BOOKS
Published by the Penguin Group: London, New York, Australia,
Canada, India, Ireland, New Zealand and South Africa
Penguin Books Ltd, Registered Offices: 80 Strand, London WC2R 0RL, England

puffinbooks.com

This edition published in Great Britain in Puffin Books 2010
1 3 5 7 9 8 6 4 2
Text and illustrations copyright © Lauren Child / Tiger Aspect Productions Limited, 2007
The Charlie and Lola Logo is a trademark of Lauren Child
All rights reserved. The moral right of the author/illustrator has been asserted
Manufactured in China
ISBN: 978-0-141-33496-7
This edition produced for The Book People Ltd,
Hall Wood Avenue, Haydock, St Helens, WA11 9UL

I have this little sister Lola.
She is small and very funny.
I am always making her jump...

But she can
NEVER
make me jump.

Lola says,
"But I really want to
make you jump, Charlie."

And I say,
"OK, Lola, but that
will **NEVER** happen."

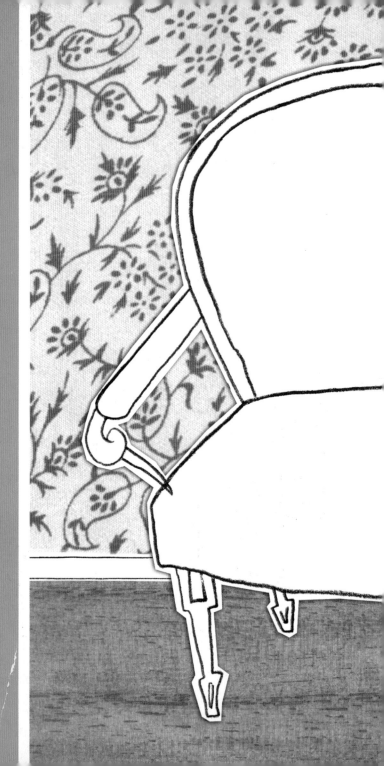

In the park,
　　Lola and Lotta scream,

"Boo!"

Lola says,
"You jumped, Charlie.
　　　　I saw you."

And I say,
　　"Don't be silly, Lola.
You'll never
　　　　make ME jump."

Later, Lola and Lotta
try to **scare** me and
Marv while we watch TV.

"Oooooohhh..."

"Oooooohhhh..."

So I say,
"Hi, Lola."
And Marv says,
"Hi, Lotta."

That night, Lola says,
    "I'm going to tell you
    a really **scary**
story about a terribly
    terrible, very old castle
full of **icky** sticky spiders."

So I say,
    "Oh, this story won't
make anyone **jump**."

But Lola says,
    "Yes it WILL, Charlie...

"Once upon a time,
there were two boys
and two
not-quite-so-biggish
small girls.
And they were lost.

They were SO lost
that they went up to a
spooky castle
to ask the way.

"They opened the door
of the **scary** castle and
went up the **creaky** stairs."

Then Lotta asks,
"Do we have to go up there?"

"Yes," says Lola.
"That's what you do in
scary stories...

And, as they followed
the biggest boy up the
creaky stairs, they heard—"

"A **ghost**!" shouts Marv.
"I'm **scared**," says Lotta.
"I'm NOT," says Charlie.

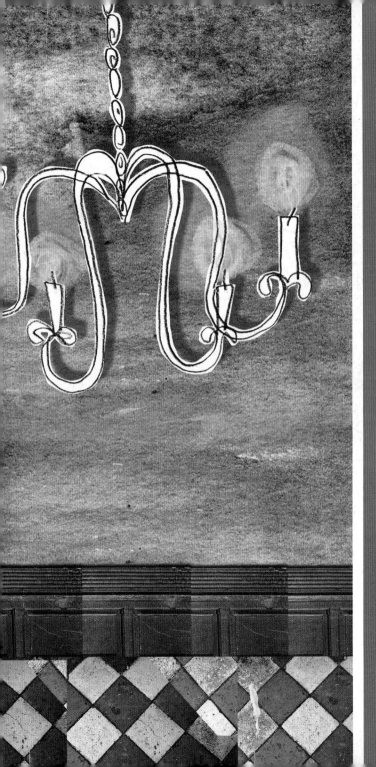

"Anyway, at the
very, very top
        of the stairs,"
says Lola,
"there was another
great
big,
ENORMOUS
door.

And, as the boy, who
        looked a bit like
Charlie, turned the handle,
        the ghosty sound
got louder and
        LOUDER...
And do you know
        who it was?" asks Lola.

"It was Twinkle!
Mrs Elmore's kitten
from next door."

"Oh, Lola!" I say.

"How is a little furry
        animal going to make
anyone jump?"

But just then...

"AHHHHH!"

I shout.
"SIZZLES, you
really made me jump."

"Hmmm," says Lola.
"Now I know
how to make
you jump, Charlie."